For Alvie and Ted,

and many thanks to David, Deirdre and Daniel.

First published 2007 by Walker Books Ltd
87 Vauxhall Walk, London SE11 5HJ

10 9 8 7 6 5 4 3 2 1

Text © 2007 Allan Ahlberg
Illustrations © 2007 Bruce Ingman

The right of Allan Ahlberg and Bruce Ingman to be
identified as author and illustrator respectively of this
work has been asserted by them in accordance with
the Copyright, Designs and Patents Act 1988

This book has been typeset in Shinn Light

Printed in China

British Library Cataloguing in Publication Data:
a catalogue record for this book is available from the
British Library

ISBN 978-1-84428-062-9

www.walkerbooks.co.uk

Previously

WALKER BOOKS

AND SUBSIDIARIES

LONDON • BOSTON • SYDNEY • AUCKLAND

Allan Ahlberg • Bruce Ingman

Goldilocks arrived home
all bothered and hot.

Previously she had been
running like mad in the dark woods.

Previously she had been
climbing out of somebody else's window.

Previously she had been
sleeping in somebody else's bed,
eating somebody else's porridge
and breaking somebody else's chair!

Previously she had been humming a tune
and having a little skip by herself in the dark woods.

Previously she had bumped into
a hurtling and older boy named ...

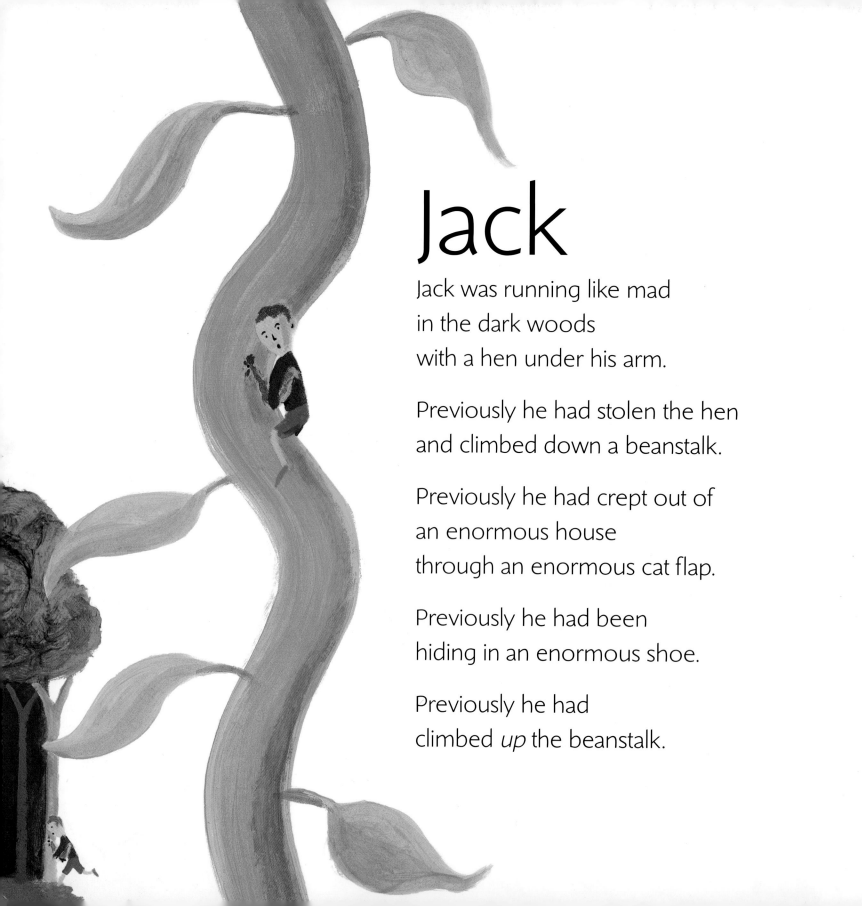

Jack

Jack was running like mad
in the dark woods
with a hen under his arm.

Previously he had stolen the hen
and climbed down a beanstalk.

Previously he had crept out of
an enormous house
through an enormous cat flap.

Previously he had been
hiding in an enormous shoe.

Previously he had
climbed *up* the beanstalk.

Previously he had swapped his cow
for some magic beans.

Previously his unhappy
(not to say desperate) mother
had sent him to market to sell the cow
because the family were so poor.

Previously he had been
playing football with his little pals.

Previously he had come tumbling down
the high hill
with his argumentative little sister ...

Jill

Jill and Jack had been
climbing the hill with a bucket.

Previously they had been
arguing over who should carry the bucket,
who had carried the bucket last time,
and, anyway, where *was* the bucket?

Previously, while eating their breakfasts
and arguing over the free gift
in the cornflakes box,
they had been said "Hallo!" to
through the open kitchen window
by a small green ...

Frog

The Frog was sitting on the windowsill
with a sorrowful look in his eye
and a crown on his head.

Previously he had been ...

A Prince

The Prince was a sorrowful young man.

Previously a wicked fairy
had put a spell on him.

Previously he had been
a cheerful young man,
eating his dinner from golden plates
and travelling his kingdom
in a milk–white Mercedes.

Previously he had fallen in love
with a disappearing girl named ...

Cinderella

Cinderella was running like mad
away from the ball.

Previously she had been dancing
her socks off with the Prince.

Previously a *good* fairy
had put a spell on *her*.

Previously she had been
dressed in rags
and slaving away for the Ugly Sisters.

Previously, on her afternoon off
and out for a stroll in the dark woods,
she had been bumped into by ...

The Gingerbread Boy

The Gingerbread Boy was being chased by
a little old man,
a little old woman,
a cow (a different cow),

a horse,
a butcher,
a baker,
a schoolful of children
and a quick brown fox.

Previously he had been
baked in an oven.

Previously he had been
a bag of flour
on a shelf
in a shop,
a field of golden corn,
a sackful of seeds.

Previously the Farmer (Goldilocks's uncle)
had ploughed the ground
and planted the seeds,
reaped and sowed,
sowed and reaped.

And previously Goldilocks herself
and Jack and Jill
and all the others,
even the little old man
and the little old woman,
had all been tiny babies ...
previously.

And all the bears were cubs.
And all the frogs were tadpoles.
And all the buckets and chairs
and ballroom floors
were planks of wood.
And all the wood was trees
... in the dark woods.

In the sun and the wind and the rain,
under the endless sky,
once upon a time ...

Previously.